Letters from PRISON

by **Kasey Parker**

DORRANCE PUBLISHING CO
EST 1920
PITTSBURGH, PENNSYLVANIA 15238

Dorrance Publishing Co
585 Alpha Drive
Suite 103
Pittsburgh, PA 15238
Visit our website at *www.dorrancebookstore.com*

ISBN: 979-8-88729-269-4
eISBN: 979-8-88729-769-9

Letters from Prison

by Kasey Parker

Contents

March
The First Letter

It's Tuesday, March 27. I can't begin to imagine why my boss wanted me and three others of my co-workers in his office even before clocking in.

My best friend Tyler is one of the people called in. He looks over at me with a blank stare, past the two other workers. I returned the stare with concern.

We all stand in Mr. Clayton's office waiting for him to come in as we all have thoughts racing through our minds. We know this cannot be good.

Mr. Clayton comes in with papers in his hand and sits at his desk. One by one, he calls us up. I'm the first one called, and Mr. Clayton hands me a pink slip. We are victims of being laid off.

Mr. Clayton stares at us, then breaks the uncomfortable silence that fills the room.

"Due to the cut of some costs, we must let some of you go. I want each one of you to know that your hard work has been nothing but appreciated. I'm truly sorry that things turned out this way."

Tyler takes off his hat and walks out the door of Mr. Clayton's office before he can finish his pity speech. He walks by me as I stand quietly. Mr. Clayton continues his speech:

"I also want to thank you for all you have done for Royals department store. Best of luck to all of you, and once again, I'm very sorry."

The remaining three of us walk out without saying a word to each other. Not like I'm close to them anyway.

I walk out the front door of my now former job. Tyler is on the bench with his hand over his face.

"Need a ride?" I ask.

"Yeah, I don't think I should be taking public transportation right now."

He grabs his bag and gets up, and we start our way to my car.

We get in as quickly as we can. I sit in the driver's seat and stare out the window with my fist to my mouth and keys in my hand. I could already feel an anxiety attack starting up.

"I depend on this job to help me pay for college…I guess I can kiss that goodbye."

"Sorry to hear that, Rachel."

"At least you still live with your parents, Tyler. I don't…this must not be a big deal to you."

"It still is with everybody else working in the house; and why do you think I rarely called out? One day of calling out I was a bum."

I started up the car and drove out of the parking lot.

Tyler was the first person I met at Royals. Him and I became friends after I got rejected for a date after he revealed to me, he was gay. Friendships do last longer than relationships anyway sometimes. I like having him around even though sometimes he is hard to look away from at times.

We pulled up in front of Tyler's house.

"Call me later, love you man."

Tyler grins at me.

"You always have since day one." He grabs his bag and gets out. He then turns around to face me again. "You know, I think Stacey should've gotten laid off, too. I mean, she has been there the same amount of time as us."

"I think so, too, or at least her hours cut. It's almost like Mr. Clayton has a thing for her."

"Listen, Rachel, I'm glad you said that because I wouldn't be surprised if he did."

"OR having an affair."

"I know we are friends and all, but truth be told… But please call me later or text."

"I will."

I drive off. It is always convenient to have a co-worker a few streets over from where I live. It is always fun to hang out with him even if I can't have him in a romantic way. But he and Stacey know how I feel about him and how I still want to be with him.

Nevertheless, I always respected his boundaries, as he was not interested in me.

I pulled up to my driveway, turned off my car, and sat trying to wrap my mind around what had just happened. I look at my clock. It's noon. My six-hour shift would be starting now. I don't understand why the workers who were there longer got laid off. It doesn't make sense to me that the longer workers got the layoff…

I get out of my car and make my way to my porch. I grab my mail and sigh. My dog Nicki is there to greet me when I walk in.

"Hey boy."

I give him a pat on the head and throw my mail on my coffee table. Nicki runs to the back door, and I let him out, grabbed my mail back off the table, and started to go through it. I can already tell there is at least one bill in the stack of envelopes. I skim through the stack.

More bills than ads, just as I thought. Water, cable, phone… There is no way this day can get any more perfect.

I came across a white envelope that caught my eye. It has my address on it but not my name. It is addressed to someone named Michelle Dale. It wasn't like me to open someone else's mail, but it is very tempting to do. I mean, it does have my address on it after all.

"What the hell? Let's make this day a little exciting," I say out loud to myself. I open it up and unfold the piece of paper that is inside.

Dear Michelle.

It's me, as my sentence is almost up. I can't wait to be reunited with you again in nine months. I know what I did is unforgivable, and I will never forgive myself for hurting you the way I did. But what's done is done. I hope one day that you can forgive me for what happened. Just felt like I had no choice. I know I said it was because I loved you. But my actions did not prove that because it hurts you. Hurt me also. When my time is up, I want to start our life together like we always planned. I know what I did was fucked up, but if you're willing to stick by me, I'll stick by you. I love you more than words can express.

Love,

Bobby

It hits me that I am reading a prison letter. I'm so hypnotized by it that I can't stop staring at it. Nicki scratches the door to be let in, and I snap out of it. This is from an actual prisoner. I am shocked and confused by this letter. This is a guy who is trying to get in touch with his girlfriend. He obviously did something so bad that he made her not want anything to do with him.

I grabbed my phone and typed a text to Tyler asking him to come over. I know he isn't busy, and this is maybe a good thing to focus on for the moment. Maybe take our minds from what just happened. I know it will take my mind off it. Knowing Tyler, he'll never confirm he is coming over—he'll just pop up. It was crazy that it ended up with me.

I study the letter again. Do I send one back or leave it alone? I am very tempted to and want to. This is a tough situation. Will he still write to me if I don't respond? Will he come after me after his time is up? A million thoughts ran through my mind. I needed an opinion. Tyler is always good at giving advice.

With my parents and sister not on speaking terms with me, I always turn to Tyler or Stacey for advice.

My doorbell rings. I check out the window for confirmation that it's not an unwanted guest. I unlock the door, and Tyler walks in.

"Safety first, right? So, what's up? Just wanted company?"

"No, more like advice. Check this out. I got this in the mail."

Tyler looks at me concerned, then unfolds the letter. His eyes widen as he reads through it.

"Wow, this is a jail letter." He hands it back to me.

"Yeah, I know. What should I write back?"

"You must reply. It's only right. Wouldn't you want to know if your letter never made it to the right person?"

"Can't leave him hanging like that."

"Just write something simple, like, 'Hey, this isn't Michelle. Best of luck with everything.' Nothing more than that."

"You're right, I guess."

I get a paper out and start my response. I don't want to get this guy's hopes up when he gets a letter back, but it must be done. I look at the envelope, and there is a return address to Brecksville Prison in the state of New Hampshire. Now I have no excuse not to respond.

Dear Bobby,

I'm writing in response to your letter. With regret, I hate to tell you your letter was never received by Michelle. I hope you get in touch with her, and best of luck when you get out. Congrats on your release.

Tyler comes over to me.

"Finish it?"

"Yes, I did. Yeah…how does this sound?"

He reads it and nods his head.

"I like it, it's perfect."

"Now to make sure it really gets mailed; I'm going to mail it on the way home."

"You don't trust me to mail it myself?"

"Let me think for a second… Uhhh, no. I know it will still be sitting here in a week. Oh, by the way Stacey sends her condolences to the both of us."

I sigh.

"Wish she called more you know? That is my bestie next to you; I guess because we're both females, we click more."

"I totally get that you want that female bond."

"Always claims to be busy though. Hey! Just like my sister."

Tyler shakes his head.: He huffs under his breath quietly.

"Have you reached out to her lately?" Tyler asks.

"No. Why bother? She never asks how I'm doing."

"Yeah, but she's pregnant, and it's a complicated one."

I argued back with him, "Why should that matter?"

Tyler shrugs his shoulders.

"I don't know. …Still your sister though. I'm going to mail this out."

"Have a good rest of your day."

"As I figured, my parents think I'm going to bum around the house now. We must hang in there, I guess."

I nod my head in agreement with him.

Tyler leaves, and I lock the door behind him. Maybe an attempted call won't hurt. After all, this is a rough pregnancy. I got my phone out and went through my contact list and got to my sister's name. Anger takes over again, and I exit my contacts list. Too busy to call me? I'm too busy to call also.

I just lost my job about two hours ago and have more important things to worry about.

April

CAN WE CHAT MORE?

It's been over a week since I sent that Bobby guy a letter back. But that is the least of my concerns right now. My main concern is getting a job. It's April 6, and bills will be piling up again soon, even though it feels like I just got done paying bills.

I sit in my den doing job applications when a knock at my door breaks my concentration. Nicki barks as I go to see who it is. I am surprised to see Tyler at my door along with Stacey. I open the door.

"Hey girl, long time no hang. Can we come in?"

"Uh, yeah. Just doing some job applications but yeah." I go back to my den as they follow me.

Tyler gives Nicki a head-scruff and says, "Hey Nick."

"Actually, it's *Nick-ee*."

"Hey, you gave him a girl's name. Gotta makes him feel like a man."

I roll my eyes and turn back to my computer.

Stacey sits between Tyler and me.

"Listen, guys, I'm sorry you got laid off, and I'm sorry I have been missing in action…just been busy. Work and school. With graduation in a year, it's stressful currently."

"We get it," Tyler says. "Right, Rachel?"

"Yeah totally. Sorry—I'm focused on these applications."

Tyler cuts in as I'm about to say something.

"Speaking of jobs, I'm starting a job next week with my uncle at his land-scaping business. I start on Monday."

I look at him with a half-smile.

"That's great to hear."

"Yeah! Way to go, bud!" Stacey gives him a shoulder punch.

"Also, he shovels in the winter, so it's basically all year around job. Hey, Rachel, tell Stacey about that letter you got like a week and a half ago."

"Letter?"

I go into my drawer, get out the letter, and hand it to Stacey.

"Got it last week from a prisoner named Bobby Lewis. Had my address on it but not my name."

As Stacey reads it, she looks just as shocked as Tyler, and I did when we first read it. Stacey sighs.

"Please tell me you did not reply."

"I did. I thought about it, and Tyler said it was the right thing to do."

"WHAT? TYLER, WHAT THE FUCK! WHY WOULD YOU TELL HER TO DO THAT?"

"It was only right, Stacey. Wouldn't you want to know if your letter never made it to its destination?"

"THIS GUY COULD BE IN JAIL FOR MURDER! YOU DON'T KNOW."

"Now would that make sense… If he was, he would NOT be getting out."

"HE'S IN JAIL BECAUSE HE'S NOT SAFE FOR SOCIETY TO BE WITH US."

I watched the two exchange words. I step out onto my porch and prop my legs up on the table. I can still hear the two arguing over what was right and wrong. I know I did the right thing.

My mail has arrived. I will go to collect it. I already noticed an envelope that is not from a company. It is the same kind of envelope that I received from the prison the first time. I fold the envelope and shove it in my pocket. There is already fighting; this will just make it worse. As much as I want to tell them, I can't. I decided to open the letter. I rip the envelope open like a child on Christmas morning.

Dear Anonymous,

This is Bobby Lewis again. I wanted to thank you for your kind, non-judgmental letter letting me know my letter never made it to my girlfriend. Thank you for your congrats and best wishes also. I refer to you anonymously because I don't know your name, so I just put your address on the envelope. If it's okay with you, I would really like to keep on chatting with you until my time is up. If so, write back if not no worries take care with everything and thanks again.

Bobby

It seems that all Bobby wants is a friend. Can't really blame the guy. I know nothing about him, but I don't mind being there in his final months. I would not mind getting to know him.

I put the letter in my pocket and went back inside. Tyler and Stacey are watching some stand-up comedy show. Things are calm. Why break that peace?

"Tyler, can you help me move my desk to the other side of my den?"

He looks at me strangely then gets up and follows me to my den.

"You want your desk moved because why…?"

"No; I do want your opinion on this."

I give him the new letter, and he reads it.

"Why not?" Tyler glances up from the letter as I interrupt his reading. "I will support you, and I assume you do not tell Stacey?"

"Please don't," I say in a desperate tone.

"Be careful with this."

"So, work Monday morning?" I ask.

"Yep, 8:00 AM."

"That's pretty early."

"Hey, we should have a get together—only because our schedules may never match up again, and I think Stacey is off this Sunday."

"So, we do something like tomorrow night."

"Or maybe even tonight."

"Is Stacey off tomorrow? Because if she is, we could totally pull this off tonight since it is only like 3:00…you could swing by at like 7:00 or 8:00."

Stacey appears from the corner.

"I heard my name, and the answer is yes."

"I guess a night off from schoolwork won't hurt."

"Yeah, let's do this tonight because I'm not off Sunday."

"I'll bring some alcohol and a few pizzas, I guess. Everyone is good with plain and pineapple?" Tyler points to all of us as he asks. We nod our heads with a little hesitation.

"I got to get home if I want to do this though because I really do have to do some schoolwork." Stacey walks out of the den. "Seven tonight guys." She closes the door.

I look at Tyler.

"Think she'll cancel like usual?"

"I understand she has a lot going on, but I don't think it's a bad thing if I ASK her to hang out once a month with me."

"I don't demand, I ask."

"I know, Rachel. I know."

"You really are a good friend to all of us. We talk highly of you all the time. You have helped us through so much. Especially me. Coming out, helping me get my license even though I don't drive now and permit also. Also supporting me when my parents didn't accept my sexuality. I appreciate our friendship very much. You don't do anything wrong by asking to hang out once a month. Nothing wrong with that. I'm going to head home though."

"Wait. Mail my letter for me?"

Tyler looked at me, shocked.

"What am I, the postal boy? … I'm just kidding! Okay, I'll wait until you're done."

I take out a piece of paper and begin my response.

"I'll make it quick."

Dear Bobby,
I accept.

"There. Simple as that." I sealed it up and handed it to Tyler.

"You already had that envelope made out in advance." I nod my head. He points at me. "Be back later."

. . .

I can hear the bad engine of Stacey's car pull in the driveway. The night came so quickly.

I unlock the door and open it for Stacey and Tyler. Stacey has the drinks in one hand while Tyler has the pizzas.

"Did you drive here together?" I ask.

Tyler walks in first and puts the pizzas down.

"Yeah, but only because of the pizzas. Did not want to carry them four blocks."

"Yeah, knowing him, he would drop them."

"Stacey, girl, you're asking for it." Tyler goes over and puts her in a playful headlock.

"Go get plates and glasses, guys. You know where they are." I go to the alcohol bag. "Three bottles? We'll be dead by the end of the night."

Stacey gives me a drama queen look.

"There are three of us. One bottle each, you know?"

"I get it now. LET'S GET THIS GOING THEN."

Bottles pop, drinks are poured, and shots are taken. Stacey and I take three shots before we surrender.

"Y'all are weak! What the hell was that?" Tyler asks. "Three? That's all you can handle?"

Stacey, with a low tolerance for alcohol, stands up, visibly drunk.

"I'm gonna go have a cigar."

It is just Tyler and I on the couch after two hours of drinking.

"We are wasted." Tyler grabs me by the arm. "Hey, are we together?"

"Sadly, no. You rejected me when I asked you out two years ago because you're gay. But I always liked you though. I think I can now tell you that I wanted to pin you up against the wall in the break room when I first saw you."

He looks at me, confused.

"Wait, what?"

"Yeah, really. You are like…adorable. Have you ever been with a girl?" I asked him.

"No need to because I know I'm gay. Don't get me wrong—you're very pretty; but I'm not sexually into you. I've never had any sexual feelings towards females; just males only."

We both hear footsteps running back in.

"RACHEL, THERE'S SOMEONE IN YOUR BACKYARD! WE'RE GONNA DIE TONIGHT!"

Tyer grabs my face and kisses me.

"Just in case we do die," he says. He grabs a fire poker and runs to the yard.

"Never mind he's gone now."

Tyler sighs and puts down the fire poker.

"Time for you to go to sleep. You're hallucinating now."

Without fighting it, she goes to the couch and lies down.

"I think I'm going to go to sleep, too," Tyler says.

"Okay. I'm going to stay down here and clean up a bit. Guest room's the first one on the right."

Tyler groggily goes up the steps as I collect the dishes. I put them in the sink and start my way upstairs and go straight to my room. I got in bed, and Nicki is already curled up at the end of my bed.

"Hey, Nicki. Too much partying for you?" I am still in utter shock that Tyler just grabbed my face and kissed me. I keep on replaying it in my mind. Did it mean something?

I'm woken up the next morning by Stacey.

"Hey, I'm heading out of here. You, okay?"

I nod. My head is hurting, and the room is fuzzy.

"Watch out for that creature."

Stacey laughs, "I vaguely remember that."

Stacey goes downstairs and quietly shuts the door. I get up and go to the bathroom. Tyler is walking out as I walk into the hallway.

"Oh, Rachel. Hi." We stand in silence for a second. "I am so sorry about last night. I guess I got a few drinks in me and went over the line. I'm very sorry."

"I know it did not mean anything. We're cool."

"One day you're going to find someone cuter than me." He makes his way to the door. "Did Stacey leave?"

"Yeah, like literally five minutes ago." I give him a handshake. "Keep in touch, Ty."

"Unlike Stacey, I will."

I close the door behind him and lean against it. I know the kiss meant nothing. Maybe it's just something he always wanted to do. I know I must move on though. Bills are due soon and will be arriving in the mail.

A week has passed. Another letter comes from Brecksville Prison. I opened the envelope and read it.

Dear Anonymous,

Thanks, I really look forward to your letters. Sorry about the delay. Been busy. But I will always get back ASAP. Let's get started then with the basics. First, what's your name? How old are you? When's your birthday? You can ask me anything. I'm an open book.

I am so nervous by his kindness.
I place the letter next to me as I continue my job: applications.

May

BOUNDARIES

With Tyler at his new job, Stacey at work and school, and me looking for a job, and just kissing my gay best friend a few weeks back, my mind is racing with thoughts of anxiety. Is Tyler avoiding me or just busy? I have not even responded to Bobby's letter. I have it still sitting where I left it. I know boundaries must be set with him. Probably, he's wondering why I haven't, but I know if I tell him why, he will understand.

I get out a piece of paper and start my response back.

Dear Bobby,

Sorry I know it's been a while a lot has been going on. But my name is Rachel. I'm 27, and yes, I already had a Birthday in January. Same questions for you. But I would like to set a few boundaries with you.

No asking for money on your books.

No sexual talk.

No personal questions.

Sometimes I like to be left alone in my thoughts. So, if I ever take long a long time to reply, don't double write to me. I'm okay and will get back to you.

Sealing it up, I am getting anxious. Will he be mad and never talk to me again for setting these boundaries with him? It's 7:00 PM. Tyler must be done with work by now. I called him.

"Hey, Rachel, let me guess: you need another letter mailed?"

"You think you can't do it?" I sigh. "Yes actually."

"This is the last time I'm doing this for you. You got to do this on your own."

Tyler meets me at my door, and I hand him the next letter.

"I set boundaries, like no asking for money or sexual talk or personal questions. Think he'll be mad?"

Tyler raises his eyebrows while looking at the envelope.

"If he is, then it's not worth it."

"Thanks, Tyler. How's work going?"

"Good, and how's your job hunt?" I roll my eyes. "I know," he tells me. "You just got to keep trying though. Something will come up." He walks off my porch.

"Be safe!" I yell.

He turns and waves with the letter in his hand.

I don't think there is anything wrong with setting those boundaries. But if I don't hear from him, I will know why. I guess for now I will just focus on me. I start my way upstairs as my biological clock starts to kick in. With all my days empty, the stress, boredom, and just normally going to bed every night makes it easier to fall asleep after Nicki's routine of going out back and eating.

I text Stacey just to check up on her:

Hey, just checking in. Hope things are going smoothly with school been a while, but I get it.

I get myself ready for bed as my phone dings to notify me for a new text.

How about having some respect? You know I'm busy with work and school.

I look at my phone and my mouth drops open. What the hell I do? All I did was ask how things are going. I start to type a reply out:

Okay, from now on, I'll only text you when you text first like we always do. Sorry.

This is the hard part about being friends with Stacey; she is unpredictable. I never know if I will get Dr. Jekyll or Mr. Hyde when I call. But then she complains when I don't reach out.

My phone dings again. It's Stacey.

I'm sorry. I have been stressed lately. Text me anytime, don't take it per-sonally. Things are good, thanks. By the way, be careful with that prisoner. Tyler told me that you're going to keep writing to him until his time is up.

I threw my phone down on my bed in disgust. I guess Dr. Jekyll has come out. I get into bed and turn my light off. Even though she apologized, I still want to wait for her or until the semester is up. Paralegal is a tough field, and she's been like this since she started.

.　　.　　.

It's been eight days since I mailed my letter to Bobby. I sit and stare at the envelope that rests upon me. I nervously open it.

> *Dear Rachel,*
>
> *I will, of course, respect your boundaries. No problem at all.*
>
> *But the answers to your questions: My name's Bobby. I'm a 33-year-old prisoner, as you know. My birthday is not until the end of December on the twenty-eighth. I'll be 34 this year. Also, I was wondering if you're okay with it. I would love to meet you before my time is up. Because you seem so kind and caring, and you would be in a safe area with guards and a glass between. If that interests you, let me know. I know it's weird to ask, but of course I'm not going to ask you for a picture.*

I am so taken back that this guy wants to meet sometime next month. I don't know what I want. It is a mixture of yes and no. I do feel a connection with him on a friendship level. I figure I'll sit on it for a while and let it sink in. I want so much to text Tyler and Stacey, but by now, they are probably tired of hearing about it. I know they are there for me though. I put the letter down, and I'm hoping for a text from Tyler or Stacey. This is one thing I really need advice on.

The day drags on as I fill out job applications. But before I know it, it's already 5:00 PM. Maybe the applications felt dragged out, not the actual day. I go to grab my phone from the living room. One new text from Tyler:

Tyler, I'm so glad you texted me. Bobby said he wants to meet next month at his cell… Should I go? He said it would be secure with guards and glass between us.

I can tell he is replying with a long response.

He said it is a secure place with guards, so why not? Go out of your comfort zone. I will drive you. My uncle could miss me for one day, but you're going to have to mail the letter yourself. I say go for it.

I was hoping he wouldn't say that. But maybe he is right. I hesitantly got out a piece of paper and started to respond.

Dear Bobby,

Yes, why not? Let me know what days you are available, and let's make it happen. Yeah, it would be good to have a face to go with the letters. I look forward to meeting you. I think it's good that we do, just so we're not total strangers. Whether or not we become longtime friends, I think it's good for both of us.

I seal it up in a pre-addressed envelope and start to go out the door to mail it. I run into the mailman as I'm walking out.

"Oh my gosh, I'm so sorry." I put my hand up.

"Oh no, you're fine." The mailman has a stack of mail "Rachel Morrison?"

"Yes," I replied. He hands my mail to me.

"You're mailing that?"

"Uh yeah."

"Let me save you a trip to the mailbox."

I hesitantly handed him the letter. "Thanks, have a good one."

"You too, Miss Morrison."

I close my door. Did I just give my mailman my jail letter? Will he really mail it, or worse, open it? I regretted it right after. I came across my letter for the college I applied for a little bit longer than a year ago. Like it really mattered at this point. I open it up anyway and read it.

Dear Rachel Morrison,

Congratulations! You have been accepted to Long Wood college for the Fall semester of this year for the following program of law.

Financial aid is still a shot. I log onto my laptop to find out if I'm eligible or not. I log on to the college's website and log into my email. There is one email, and it already looks not promising. I take a deep breath and open it. It is a rejection email. Just read the first six words: "We regret to inform you of

I click out of it and just cover my face as I breakdown. College dreams go up in flames. What else can go wrong?

I decided to write Bobby another letter with a date for a possible meet up. After all, I guess I could use something to get out of the house and my mind off everything. I am excited and nervous at the same time and did want to meet Bobby. But it is so nerve wracking. Just getting out paper and starting is giving me an anxiety attack. Am I really going to do this?

Dear Bobby,

I'm available any day of the week. How about June 12th? So, pick a day and I'll plan it. My number is area code -000 3311 that's in case any-thing comes up like day of and a letter doesn't get to me in time.

I package up the envelope and go out the door to mail it off. Nicki comes up with his leash.

"Okay, we can go for a walk while I'm at it." I put the leash on Nicki and started my way to the mailbox at the end of the street. I reach the mailbox and slip it in. I text Tyler while Nicki looks for an area to go to the bathroom.

Hey, so June 12th is the day. I hope so.

Okay, sounds good I'll put it on my calendar and take off in advance. By just assuming that date works.

For some reason, Bobby was brought to me. I'm not quite sure why though.

As May is nearing the end, all bills are paid but still no job. I know the visit in the next two weeks is coming up possibly, but all this during the challenging process really isn't interfering. I don't need a hectic life to be successful.

June

THE MEETING

It's June 12, the day of the visit. I'm a nervous wreck, and Tyler is already on his way. I am happy that he said he would drive me, as I know if I had to drive myself, I would back out.

I got a knock at my door. I open it, and it's Tyler's arrival.

"Hi there, are you all ready to go?"

"Just a minute." I look in the mirror to adjust my hair. "Okay, now I am."

I walk out behind Tyler and lock up my house. We get in my car, and he takes the driver's side.

"Okay this is it. We are approximately about a half hour away."

"I got a voicemail this morning, hoping for a cancellation."

"Oh damn, Rachel." We pulled out onto the street. "I guess you don't want to talk to calm your nerves?"

"No, not really," I responded.

"Just think of it this way: He's probably just as nervous as you are."

I nod my head.

"He must be" "There's no way he can't be.

"Not sure if I'm going to be allowed in the parking lot or not, so how long do you think you'll be?"

"Forty-five minutes to an hour, I assume."

"Okay if I am kicked out, I'll time it."

"So, any advice?"

"Uh, just be yourself? Like that's all I can really say."

"I'm just saying an hour because of all the preparation I'll have to do when I walk in."

"True. We're getting closer by the way."

We pull into a long path of road that leads to the prison. This is such a completely different world. Barbed wire fences and concrete walls are so weird.

"Okay…this is it."

"Don't be nervous."

I get out and start my way to the front door. A guard is there to greet me.

"NAME PLEASE," she says in a stern tone.

"Rachel Morrison."

"Go in, they'll lead you from there."

I walk in through the metal detector and take everything out of my pocket and hand the bucket to the guard. My ID is the only thing. The guard checks it, then hands it back to me.

"Who are you here for?" the desk guard asks.

"Bobby Lewis."

The desk guard checks his list.

"Rachel?"

"Yes, that's me."

"Please fill out this form: name, age, and relationship to the prisoner, and we'll lead you."

I fill out the form and hand it back to him.

"Thank you," he says.

The wall guard takes me and brings me to a room full of phones and chairs. He sits me down at phone number four.

"Just a a minute."

I can hear footsteps coming up. I take a deep breath. I am ready for this.

He appears from the hallway. A white guy with black hair and a beard. About 6 feet, with tattooed arms in an orange jumpsuit, he sits down at the phone and points to it. We each pick up a receiver.

"Hi Rachel," Bobby says.

"Hi Bobby," I reply.

"How are you?" he asks.

"Good; just a little nervous. How about yourself?"

"Understood. I'm good, just got done working. I wash dishes for a quarter a day."

"Okay, not bad, I guess!" I let out a laugh.

"So, let's get to it. What would you like to know about me? I will be honest from the gate."

"Why are you serving time?

"I knew that question would come up eventually… So, my girlfriend and I were struggling with food. One night, we had an argument, and I went out around 11:00, and I saw this old couple walking, and I went up to them, put a gun to their head, and demanded their money. They gave it, and I spent it on food, and that got me two years in here."

"Oh, wow that really…sucks. I'm sorry to hear that; like, I really am. You don't look like the type of person that would do that."

"I did though."

"Since you told me your story, it's only fair if I tell mine. I have both parents, a sister, a brother-in-law, and I have a niece or nephew on the way. I also have the two greatest friends in the world. One drove me here. Just got laid off from my job. I got accepted into my dream college, but all the money I saved up for college is going towards bills. I am not able to get financial aid. I don't talk to my family because they're mad because my late aunt left me her house, and everybody believes that my sister should've gotten the house because she's married." "But my aunt thought it would be good if I got the house."

"All that is very unfortunate. You don't know what your sister is having, boy or girl?"

"Too early still."

"You're going to have to call your sister at some point. You're talking to someone who lost their only sister at 15. Tomorrow is not promised. I have two brothers, but they have got that twin thing going on. Forgive those who are wrong…even if they're not sorry for their actions. She died in a car crash."

"It's been over a year since we talked," I say. "I found out she was pregnant through my parents."

"I get it you're stressed about a job and school," Bobby continues.

"She should reach out too—" I start.

"You're both acting immature; just being stone cold with you. Call maybe once a week until she answers. Just keep trying." He changes the subject: "What was your job?"

"Customer service with my two best friends. The one who drove me here actually got laid off with me."

"Tell him I said thank you."

"We accidentally kissed last month while we were drunk."

"Oh, you like each other?"

"I like him. I always have, and he knows it… But he's, uh, gay. I don't know why it hurt me so much. He did apologize, but still though…"

"Because it meant something to you," Bobby replies. "Listen you can have sex or kiss anybody—friend, ex…hookup and have it not meant a thing. You're more hurt because it meant more to you than him. You have good friends. Don't let them go. When is your sister due?"

"November. But it's a complicated pregnancy"

"Even more of a reason to call."

Now it's my turn to change the subject.

"I'm going away on the Fourth of July. That should be fun."

"Oh cool. That's in like three weeks. By the way, you did give me your number. Can I call sometimes then?"

"Absolutely."

"Hate to cut you off, but I must do my workout now. I set a schedule for myself. But it was such a pleasure meeting you. Thank you so much for coming out. I look forward to reading more letters."

"Same thanks for having me."

"For sure. Of course. Take it easy now."

We hung up the phones, and the guard walked me out.

"You did great," he tells me, "I saw you were nervous. It's always tough though."

The guard walks me through to the main door as the metal detector guard let me out.

"Have a good rest of your day," the front the guard says.

I see Tyler in the driveway.

"Hey, I'm back," I say as I enter the car. I startle him.

"Oh my God! You scared me!" Tyler puts his hand across his chest. "So how did it go?"

"Pretty good. We talked about the past, present, future, family and all that. Also, I know why he's in there."

"Wait, you didn't already know?"

"I thought it would be more appropriate in person to ask, not through letters."

"I get it, yeah. I guess it would have been awkward."

"Armed robbery of an elder couple for food. Long story short."

Tyler nods his head and says, "A little scary, but don't tell Stacey that."

"He also told me to call my sister."

"ANOTHER ONE!" Tyler said. "We're all telling you to do that, so…"

We start our drive back to town.

"You know calling my sister isn't as easy as everybody thinks. Last thing she said to me was, 'Never speak to me again.'"

We stop at a red light, and Tyler glances over at me.

"I know but be the bigger person. It doesn't take a lot of energy to text someone. I know there's a lot of tension, but just try."

Tyler starts to drive as the light turns green.

"Why try to mend a bridge that I didn't even burn? Give me one good reason."

"Because it's your sister. Just give it a thought at least." Tyler drives up his street, and he gets out of the driver's side. "You got it from here, Rachel?"

"I got it."

I get in the driver's seat and drive the few streets over, back to my house, and walk up my porch. My mail has been delivered. There is a letter from Bobby. I already knew I was going to write him as soon as I got home.

> *Dear Bobby.*
> *Thank you for having me today. I really enjoyed it. Thanks again.*

I put the letter in my mailbox for the mailman to take, even though mail was already delivered today. What's the difference? I just want to relax after this long, weird day and get back to job hunting. I know Bobby has priorities, and he wouldn't be writing weekly, but I always want the best for people and their futures, even for Tyler and Stacey. Plus, it gives him something to do. I'm more than just a random person to write to. I would never expect someone to put me first.

.   .   .

It's been two weeks since the visit. Bobby has responded to my last letter. I haven't even noticed Bobby hasn't written to me since I am so stressed about jobs and bills, it just totally slipped my mind. I haven't even checked my mail thoroughly in the past week or so. My focus is getting a job. Having Bobby is just a bonus.

I grabbed my mail and noticed one letter.

Dear Rachel,
Sorry for the lateness again. But I noticed it's almost the Fourth of July.
I hope you have a wonderful holiday and stay safe.

I like that I have someone to talk to who is older, and someone other than just Tyler and Stacey. Bobby has a lot of experience in life already while Tyler and Stacey are only 24. Some things, they just didn't understand about life or me.

July
A Chance for Romance

It's the Fourth of July. As I wait at Tyler's house to drop off Nicki and get picked up by Stacey, Tyler walks downstairs.

"Oh Rachel, I did not know you were here already."

"I just got here about 10 minutes ago."

"Oh, where are my parents?"

"In the yard with Nicki. Tyler nods. Be right back I'm going to let them know I'm leaving."

I go out front and wait for Stacey's arrival. I am looking forward to a night with the trio.

Tyler comes from out back and sits next to me on the front steps and sits in silence.

Stacey pulls up in the driveway.

"HEY GUYS, HOP IN! WE GOT A LONG RIDE…KINDA!"

Tyler gets in the back, and I get in the front.

"Happy Fourth! Yes, I'm over excited," Stacey says.

"Same to you," I say.

"I'm glad I'm not in the front," Tyler interjects. "I'm going to block you out with headphones. Have fun up there, Rach."

Tyler puts headphones on and slouches against the window.

We are on our way to the beach bash.

"So, since Tyler is sleeping, how is everything with your jail buddy?"

"My jail buddy? Uh, good… I'm being careful, like you told me."

"Good. Hate to see you end up dead."

"He told me through a letter why he's serving time. Don't freak out, okay? He robbed an old couple to buy food."

"Oh, that's…pretty dark," Stacey says.

"I know it is. But he got punished for it."

"Did he ever reach his girlfriend?"

"Don't think he did, I didn't ask him. Now I'm curious though. How's school going?"

"Going good, thanks for asking. A year until graduation, then living my dream job as a paralegal."

"I'm happy for you, really. I'm glad you got the opportunity to go to college…yeah, I got accepted into the college, but denied for financial aid."

"DAMN. That sucks. They say why?"

"I'm sure they did, but I didn't read the rest of the letter, just read what we regret."

"I guess that's all you need to read, huh?"

"Yes, very self-explanatory."

"Just keep trying."

We pull up to the boardwalk where music is blaring, bonfires are lit, and people are enjoying the night. We get out and start our way to the beach, where all the action is.

"Lock the shit out of your car," Tyler tells Stacey. She locks it up and we start our way up.

We are each automatically handed a beer as we walk on the beach.

"I guess we look of age," Tyler says.

We sit on a log and crack open the beers and watch all the people who are already drunk.

I look across the log, and there's a guy with black hair and a clean-shaven face staring back at me. I give a nervous wave. It looks like he is with three other guys.

One of the hostesses comes up to us and handed us a box of sparklers.

"Don't worry; everything's free here, "she says.

As Stacey is talking to me, I keep on staring at the guy, and he lights up a sparkler. I keep track of where he's going, and I start to follow him.

=I go to where he is on the other side and tap him on the shoulder. He turns around and smiles.

"Hey there," he begins. "I saw you across the bonfire."

"Yeah, I saw you, too," I say in reply.

"Who are you here with?" he asks.

"Two of my friends."

"Oh, so that guy with the blonde is NOT your boyfriend?"

"Oh, noooo! Just my friend."

"Cool cool cool. Would you want to watch the show together on the boardwalk?" he asks.

"I should tell my friends first," I reply.

"I'll be here waiting for you."

I walk over to Tyler and Stacey.

"Go!" They both shoo me away.

I go back to the guy. We walked up to the boardwalk, and he handed me a sparkler.

"I'm scared of those actually," I confide.

He takes it back and lights it himself.

"Now just hold it out," he says. "So where are you from?" he asks. "I'm sorry; I didn't get your name… Let's start with that."

"My name's Rachel, and I'm from Engleton."

"No way! You're lying! I'm from there, too! I live next to the pizza shop. By the way my name is Josh, and those guys are my adoptive brothers technically. We should hang out sometime." He adds, "I think you're really pretty."

I blush.

"Thank you. You're cute too."

The show starts, and we both lean over the rail.

The fireworks light the sky up. Josh puts his arm around me. I look over at him, and he motions a phone gesture with his hand. I bring my phone out, and he puts his hand out as a sign to *hand it to me.* He puts his number in and leans close to me.

"Friday night?" he asks. I nod my head with a grin. "I want to get to know you, even if it's just friends."

The sky lights up with a million fireworks at once.

"Must be the finale," Josh says.

"Yeah, it must be," I concur.

The air fills with clapping and cheering. Tyler and Stacey sneak up behind me and grab me by the shoulder.

"Oh, hey guys! Enjoy the show?" I ask.

"Yeah, not bad." Tyler replies.

"Uh, guys, this is Josh. Josh, these are my best friends, Tyler and Stacey."

He puts out his hand and shakes each of their hands. I continue, "We live in the same town."

Josh nods and says, "I do." Then, "I should get back to my brothers… Friday night: Let's make plans. Nice meeting you guys. Happy Fourth!"

"HOLY SHIT, COME ON! WE HAVE TO GET BACK TO THE CAR." Stacey runs to the lot and unlocks the car. "THIS IS SO EXCITING! I WANNA HEAR ABOUT IT."

Tyler gets in the back, and I get in the front seat.

"So, tell us, "He says.

"His name is Josh. He lives in Engleton, and we're going to go out in two days…on Friday."

"Where to?" Tyler asks.

"Not sure yet… Let me take the wheel, Stacey. You good to drive?"

She pushes my hand away as I go to grab the wheel.

"Yes, I'm okay. Let's get home. But CONGRATS, GIRL!"

She starts the car up, and we start our way home.

"So did you call your sister yet?" Tyler asks.

"No, because it isn't that easy, Tyler."

"You don't even know what she's having because it's been so long," he starts.

"Not my kid," I snap.

"Yeah, but it is your niece or nephew though at the end of the day."

"The worst that could happen is she doesn't pick up," Stacey says.

"Stacey, just focus on the road."

"Even Bobby says the same."

"You know what, guys, I will… But know she won't pick up."

"I know it will be awkward, but give it a go," Stacey says.

We drove back to town to Tyler's house.

"You going to walk it?" Stacey asks.

"Yeah, thanks, Stacey."

"Text you guys tomorrow!"

"She won't," Tyler says as he unlocks the door.

Nicki runs up to me with a bark.

"Thanks for watching her, guys."

"Oh, no problem," Tyler's mother says in return. I give Tyler a hug and start my walk home with Nicki. "Good night, guys."

I return to an empty house. I have been so busy; I haven't even checked the mail I received yesterday. I saw a letter from Bobby. I can't wait to tell him about Josh. It is the first letter since the visit.

Sleep is calling. I unpack Nicki's bag and open Bobby's letter. I am very eager to tell him about everything.

> *Dear Rachel,*
>
> *I know it's been a minute. Just wanted to say I hope you have a fun and safe trip. I've been working to get used to working when I get out…if I can land a job that is.*

I put the letter down on my table and went up to bed. Calling my sister crosses my mind, but I just am not ready to. No one understands my situation. I will go at my own pace, as slow as I need to.

Morning comes. I grabbed my phone, and I saw a text from Josh. I guess he is confirming a place for tomorrow. I open it.

> *Hey Rachel. It's Josh. Listen, I'm going to have to push our date back for a few weeks. There's something I didn't tell you last night. I have a grandfather who's on his deathbed, and between work and him, he's kind of like my focus right now. Hope you understand.*

I am just a little saddened, but I understand and send him a sympathy text, then go downstairs.

I let Nicki out and sent a group text to Tyler and Stacey about my canceled date. Stacey replies first:

> *Sorry to hear that… A few weeks is kind of long, but I guess it's reasonable.*

A text from Tyler then comes through.

> *I guess I just support him at this time.*

I put my phone down and started my letter to Bobby.

> *Dear Bobby,*
> *My trip went great. I met a guy named Josh at the show. Get this: He lives in my town! Crazy, right? We were supposed to go out on Friday the 6th, but his grandfather is in his final days, so it's pushed back. No rush to reply, I get you are busy now.*

I wait for Nicki to come back in, so I can go and mail it. I called Nicki in and gave him his breakfast. I get my shoes on and start my run to the mailbox. As Bobby works now, I know weekly letters will not be as often. I dropped the letter in and headed back home.

It's been two weeks now since Josh's grandfather prepared to leave the world. I have been texting him throughout all of this as I sit in my den.

I got a knock at my door. It's Tyler and Stacey. The expressions on their faces look mad and disgusted.

"Yes?"

"Yeah, hi," Tyler starts. "We're just wondering, why are you subjecting yourself to a guy who doesn't give a shit about you?"

I looked at him confused.

"Do you understand his grandfather is on his deathbed?" "Deathbed."

"We get that, but if he really liked you, he would make time to text you." Stacey says. "I'm starting to think he's playing you."

"Whatever, guys. Just get out."

"Fuck this, Stacey. She doesn't want to hear what a piece of shit he is, so let her learn the hard way. You belong with him because you're both shitty.

"When we got laid off, you didn't even ask me if I was okay. You were just concerned about yourself. Tell Stacey what you said. Go on, tell her or I will." I Stood silent with an anxiety attack coming on and I think they both knew it.

"Okay I will then. She said you should gotten laid off and you're having an affair with the boss to get more hours."

"You said that, too, Tyler."

They both walk out. Were they really mad over a guy who was honestly busy with life?

I shake my head and grab my mail. Bobby has sent a letter. I am glad to see a letter in my stack of mail.

>*Dear Rachel,*
>
>*That's great to hear but sad about his grandfather. I'm sure he'll go out with you as soon as he can. Do your friends like him? Thanks for understanding. Get back to you as soon as I can.*

I couldn't reply; not right now. I just lost my two best friends. Josh is going through his own situation, and it was the same with Bobby. Josh could not control what was going on right now.

August
Do You Forgive Yourself?

It's August 1. I haven't heard from Tyler or Stacey in five days. I have never felt so alone. My family hates me, and now my two best friends hate me, too. Tonight, is my first date with Josh. His grandfather still has not passed, but his brothers want him to go out for a night.

I lie on my couch and scroll my social media page. I pop up when I saw something unexpected.

Tyler and Stacey are posting hateful things about me. I have been nothing but a good friend to them over the past two years. It's weird: They always praised me, saying I am a great friend; now all of a sudden, I'm not?

I'm in utter shock as I read on and on. All this had to do with Josh. Why is Tyler even involved? This has nothing to do with him. I can understand Stacey being upset about this, but not Tyler. Tyler must remember that he said the same about Stacey also. They don't have to like Josh, but they could support me in who I want to date. They are egging each other on.

Do I stay with Josh or let him go? I don't think my friendships can be fixed anyway because this is not just about Josh but what I said and not being considerate after the layoff.

I start my reply to Bobby on my couch.

Dear Bobby,

I hate to say it, but my two best friends are mad at me now and saying hateful things online of how horrible I am when I've been nothing but a good friend to them. This is because Josh keeps canceling on me. Also, they say I'm inconsiderate because after the layoff, I was not concerned about Tyler.

We have a date tonight (8/1, depending on when you get this). Will let you know how it goes and keep you updated about this.

I seal it up and throw it on my table. I should have waited until after the date to make a reply out; but I can always write another out.

I look at my clock, and it's 4:00 PM. Josh is due over at 6:00.

I am already dressed and ready to start something with this guy. We have not seen each other since the Fourth of July, but I know a connection is there.

Josh pulls up in his blue convertible and gets out.

"Hey there!" he greets. "Finally, right?"

"Yeah!" I say in reply.

Josh walks onto my porch and gives me a hug. He's holding a bag of sushi in his hand.

"Come on in!" I tell him

We walk in and sit on the couch.

"Would you like a beer or anything?" I offer.

"I guess just some water," he replies.

I bring him a glass of water as he unpacks the food.

"So, my friends are being assholes—the ones you met—because they think you're playing me, and they're saying hateful shit on the internet about me all down my page. I know why it took so long to go out with me… I get it. I know you're a great guy."

He glances at me and says, "And you're a great woman. Don't worry about them; just enjoy the night with me." He leans in and kisses me. I blush. "Come on let's eat. I want to get that in as soon as possible!" he says.

"What do you do for work again? Mechanic, right?"

"Yeah, a mechanic. And you just got laid off, right?"

"Yes unfortunately." I say in reply.

"You'll get a job somewhere eventually. May take some time though."

We continue eating as the night goes on…

"By the way," Josh begins, "I don't know when I will be available again. I'm sorry. I really am trying my best to hang out with you. But let's not start anything until all this is over."

I smile and respond, "Okay. No rush."

He looks at his watch.

"Oh shit. It's 11:00? I gotta get going; I got work at 7:00. I will text you though."

I walk him to the porch, and he kisses me goodbye.

"I had a great time, and I hope you did, too—and enjoyed the food!"

"I did! And I'm looking forward to us."

"Goodnight Rachel."

He gets in his car and pulls out of my driveway.

I go back in, and Nicki is waiting to be let out. I let him out and grab my phone and go back on social media. Surprisingly, there are no more hateful things. I go on my friends list, and I am now off their lists!

I threw my phone down in disgust. They literally kept me on their lists just to harass me!

I got a piece of paper and began my second letter to Bobby.

Dear Bobby.

The date went good. His grandfather still has not died. But he wanted to go out for a night. He said let's wait until all this is over to start something serious. I get it though it's a tough time for him and his family.

Tyler and Stacey kept me on their friends lists just to harass me. I'm now off their lists. How mature! They were just trying to get a reaction out of me. I just hope that things get okay over time with Josh and I and my friends. I do miss them though.

I seal it up and throw it on my table with the other one. They can wait until tomorrow. It is 11:00 at night, after all; and anyway, Nicki has come in, and I am locking up to end my night.

I start my way up to bed, so over everything with Tyler and Stacey at this point. But there is nothing I can do even though they hate me now. I still want their friendship. Or maybe I am just used to having them around…? Even if I didn't hear from Stacey for months at a time sometimes, it was a security thing.

I woke up the next day to my alarm. It's 11:00 AM. I want nothing to do with the world after last night. I look at my phone, and there are no texts from Josh or anyone else. I am thankful to have Bobby in my life, but with his busy schedule now with him preparing to come back out into the world, I didn't want to become a burden to him. He's been so kind to me, and I don't want him to think I am just full of drama.

At least I don't have to see anymore hate things online from my now former friends. Our friendship is over. I screwed up, and I accepted that. That's just life sometimes. You gain and lose people all through life.

I go downstairs and see the two letters that I wrote to Bobby. I want to get them out as as soon I can. I put my shoes on with the letters in hand and started my way to the mailbox. It's a nice day out; not too hot for a summer day.

I walk the few streets down to the mailbox to mail off the letters. As I walk there, I have some hesitations about dropping the letters in the mailbox. Will Bobby hate me for venting too much?

My anxiety is rising as I reach the mailbox. I breathe deep and drop them in the mailbox. People have always made me feel like I am an annoying or a drama-filled person.

We all have setbacks occasionally… Can't expect a perfect life; that's just not realistic.

When I return, I'm greeted at the door by Nicki. My only companion left. "Sorry, Nicki. I just wanted to get those letters mailed."

I open the door and fill his bowl as he goes out. I sit at my kitchen counter and think. I don't know, and my mind is all over the place.

All I want is for things to go back to the way they were. I want my friends, family, and job back. The thing I need the most right now is support, and I have no one to turn to. I know Bobby will cut me off after those letters I just mailed.

I get my laptop out and keep my mind busy with job applications. It has been five months since the layoff, and I've not had one call back yet. I know I must keep going with applications. Money is starting to run a little low. It is now desperation time.

I have not heard from Josh in four days now. I sit with another letter from Bobby. I plan to stop by Josh's house when I make my reply out, just to make sure everything is okay.

Dear Rachel,

I'm sorry to hear about your current situation. But congrats on your new romance. If it's okay, I would like to hear more about this fight you had with them. I don't mind listening. I mean, in jail or not, vent to me anytime.

I got a little emotional as I read his letter. Someone who will listen! I began my reply right away.

> *Dear Bobby,*
>
> *Thanks, I appreciate that. I just hate how they praise me one day, and the next day, they don't. Like, I was there for Tyler with coming out to his parents, helping him getting his permit AND license, and that permit took a while also. And helping Stacey out with schoolwork with her college—and I also helped out with her paying for books since she was broke at the time, and this is what I get?*

I put the letter in an envelope and started my way to mail it. I am also nervous about going to Josh's house on the way back.

I have anxiety all the way to the mailbox, drop in the letter, and make a detour to Josh's house. I can see Josh's house in the distance. His car is in the driveway.

I ring the doorbell. A brown-haired girl answers the door

"Oh, hi. Is Josh here? Who are you, his sister?"

The girl looks at me with a confused look and replies, "I'm his girlfriend of eight months. Who the hell are you? You must be the girl from the Fourth of July. Yeah, we were broken up at the time, but then I found out he was with someone else, and we got back together."

Josh comes to the door.

"So, this is why you have not been calling me," I say.

He looks at me.

"I'm sorry."

The girl closes the door as hard as she can, and I walk away in tears and heartbroken. I doubt his story now about his grandfather. Was it even true?

I ran back home as fast as I could, in tears. I can't believe this! I am upset and angry. Tyler and Stacey were right, I am so embarrassed. I can't even turn to them now. Plus, they would just laugh anyway and say, "we told you so

I am having a panic attack. I unlock my door and go over to my couch and start hyperventilating. My family and friends hate me; my boyfriend was cheating the whole time with an ex; money is running low…no job still. I've never felt so alone. Truly alone.

Nothing is going right anymore. Everything has been falling apart since my aunt died and my family stopped talking to me.

I breathe deeply and start to come down from my attack. Life is too much right now.

Nicki comes and curls up beside me as my attack comes down.

.   .   .

It's been a week since the breakup with Josh. It's August 12. I awoke to the sound of my phone vibrating. I look at the ID. It's a number that I don't recognize. I answer it. A voice comes over the other end:

"This is Brecksville Prison. Do you accept these charges? Please say yes or no…"

I'm hesitant for a moment, then I decide: "Yes, I accept."

Bobby's voice comes from the other end.

"Hey," he says. *"I got your letter, but I wanted to call, too. Maybe… I don't know, we can talk more about it. If you want to, that is."*

"I found out Josh was lying about his grandfather. He went back to his ex. His girlfriend was there today when I went over to check on him. She answered, and he could say was 'sorry,' then she slammed the door!" I confide.

"I'm sorry," Bobby says. *"I know you must be feeling broken."*

"I am I can't stop crying, and now my friends hate me, too!"

"Look," Bobby begins, *"I know it must hurt… Like, I'm going through it right now with Michelle. But you put your focus on your sister and her pregnancy, whether your niece or nephew is going to make it in November. You listening to me, Rachel?"* he prompts. *"Also, you sound like you have been a great friend. Okay, so maybe you were not as considerate as you could be after the layoff, but you're not perfect."*

"Honestly, I wasn't," I agree.

"You admit it!" Bobby says.

"I'm not proud. I have been kind of shitty, and maybe they are hurt. I've been horrible to them."

"Let me ask you: Do you forgive yourself?" Bobby says.

"…No. I can't."

"You have to in order to move on," he says. *"Tell you what: You need to write them letters, just so you have a clear conscience. If they answer, great! If they don't,*

then at least you know that you tried. I did, and now I know that Michelle wants nothing to do with me."

"I think you're right," I tell him.

"I know I'm right, hun," Bobby insists. *"You know you were a good friend for the most part."*

"Then why do I still feel guilty?"

"You're letting them make you feel that way," he explains. *"Yeah, maybe you weren't considerate with the whole job thing, but it was a one-time thing out of how many years?"*

"Two long years…"

"Hang in there, okay?" Bobby says. *"But listen, I got to go eat some lunch. I'll make sure to write a letter tonight, okay? Bye for now."*

"Thanks for calling. Perfect timing. Have a good lunch, Bobby."

I hung up. Maybe he is right. I'll send letters to Tyler and Stacey. But as for my sister, it is time for a call.

I dial her number in my contact list. It rings six times before her machine picks up, so I leave a message:

"Hey, it's your sister, give me a call when you get a chance. Love you."

I hang up and sit and think about the phone call I had with Bobby about everything. Is it worth a shot even at this point?

September

LETTERS OF APOLOGY

Not hearing from Tyler and Stacey is weird. I want to make things right; or at least try. It's September 3. There sit three letters from Bobby. I have not replied ever since our phone call. He is not wrong about making letters. I tore open the letters from Bobby.

Dear Rachel,

It was nice talking to you today. Take your time to reply; no rush. Maybe take some time to yourself. I don't mind.

Dear Rachel,

I hope everything is going good with you.

Dear Rachel,

I assume you are taking time to yourself like I suggested. If you are, no problem, but I am getting a little concerned. I don't want to call and sound like a crazy stalker, so just making everything is okay. I just want to make sure you're okay and all.

I get my paper out and start my letters to those who I hurt in my life. Since I am blocked, I send each a personal letter.

Dear Tyler,

It's Rachel. I want to start with, I'm sorry for not considering your feelings after the layoff. I should have asked how you were doing through that time. That was wrong of me to do to a friend. I want to apologize because it's the right thing to do. I never meant to smother you with my needs or make you feel like you were responsible for helping me through my problems.

Dear Stacey

It's Rachel. I want to start with, I'm sorry for what I said. I was upset at the time and angry. Not with you but with the situation. That was wrong of me to do to a friend. I want to apologize because it's the right thing to do. I never meant to smother you with my needs or make you feel like you were responsible for helping me through my problems. Even though you don't think I care about your schooling, I do care, which is why I didn't reach out to you. You're like Dr Jekyll and Mr. Hyde—don't know which one I'm going to get if I DO reach out to you. Sometimes you go a little crazy on me.

Now, a letter for my sister…

Dear Rose,

It's Rachel. I called about a month ago. I hope that one day we can put all of this behind us and move on. Aunt Rita would not want us fighting; she would want us to get along, especially for the birth of your child. I want to hold my niece or nephew and be part of their life. I know this pregnancy has not been an easy one. Love you. Hug Mom and Dad for me.

I seal it up and add it to the other two letters. I grab another blank paper and write Bobby.

Dear Bobby,

Yes, I've been good; just wrapped up in my thoughts for a while.

I just got done writing my letters. But we will live our lives as we wait for them if they decide to reply.

I start my trip down to the mailbox. As I approach it, I notice Tyler and Stacey walking down the street. I slip the letters in and start to run back home until I reach the next street. I look back, and there is no sign of them.

 They aren't anywhere.

.   .   .

It's September 17—bill day. I am on my last bill.
It is official: I am now down to $43 dollars.
I open my letter from Bobby.

Dear Rachel,

Glad to hear that. I know it hurts, but friends come and go all through life. And why would you want them back in your life after what they did to you all over the internet? You don't need that. But remember: Stand your ground. No one can make decisions for you but you. You are a good woman and a good friend and a good future aunt. All these things that were said about you online aren't true at all, remember that.

I just cannot do it anymore. I have no job, income, family, or friends to help me out through this.

I go to my cabinet, grab a bottle of vodka and pour myself a glass, then go over to my couch. I cannot tell Bobby about this because he might think I am asking for money. Time to myself sounds good…

As if I had a choice anyway.

October
Fear of Falling

It's October 4. I sit at a table. An old bartender comes over.

"I need your ID first."

I took my ID out and handed it to him. He studies it then hands it back to me.

"Any kind of beer, I don't care what kind."

He goes and grabs a can of beer, then puts it down in front of me.

"Five dollars."

I gave over a $5 bill and cracked open the beer. I take a few big gulps, and before I know it, it's gone. I go to the fridge, grab a six pack, and bring it to the front.

"That'll be $6.90 please." I handed him a ten and grabbed my six pack of beer.

"Keep the change."

I walk into my house and put the case of beer in the fridge. I know this beer isn't going to last long. Being a lightweight helps a lot.

My mail sits on my kitchen table. I hate looking at it. I then see a letter from Bobby sticking out from the middle. I opened another beer, but I'm already a little tipsy from the bar.

> *Dear Rachel,*
>
> *I hope things are going good with you. Any word from anyone yet? Remember I'm here if you want to talk. We're kind of in the same boat here. I know I can talk to you, too, and that's what friendship is—when you stick with them through thick and thin and it's never too much. I'm a shoulder to lean on.*

I cannot tell him about my financial situation, especially after I told him not to ask me for money on his books. Maybe if I explain, he will know that I am not asking, just venting. But I still don't think it's okay.

> *Dear Bobby,*
> *My money is running low. Let's just leave it at that.*

No word from Stacey, Tyler, or Rose.

But I have bigger things to worry about, even if it is family. I am tipsy but want to get this letter out and walking around drunk could get me arrested.

I go out to my porch and place it in the mailbox for the mailman to take in the morning. I am so ready for bed even though it is only 9:00.

I wake up the next morning groggy. It's 1:00 PM, and Nicki is scratching at the door to be let out. I open the door and follow Nicki downstairs and let him out back.

I look at my bills and rub my face out of stress. I am now down to $31. I have money in my aunt's savings, which is only $3,000.

I open another beer along with my bills. All of them are so expensive.

Running low on food is another concern. I go to my food app on my phone and order things that are cheap but filling. I am in no condition to go out. I need my friends and family for support. Just any kind of human contact… Bobby is around but just wanting the comfort of a text or call.

I grab another beer and chug it as if I am at a party being challenged to chug down a drink. A half hour goes by, and I'm tipsy. With a knock at my door, I barely had the ability to even stand.

My food has always. I get up to open the door and pay the guy. I opened the door, and the guy handed me my three bags.

"Hey, that'll be $29.30."

I look at him and laugh.

"Thirty…31…32…33…"

"I got a lot to do today, can I just have my payment"? I take out my final dollars and give them to him. He walks away without a word.

That is, it: I am now out of money.

I grab the bags that consist of soups and put them in the cabinet without taking them out of the bag even. This includes three cans of Nicki's food. I

I grab another beer from the fridge and open it. I do not want to lose the drunkenness. The problems are easier to handle. I am happy, calm, and anxiety-free when alcohol is in me.

There is nothing I can do at this point. I go out and collect my mail. Another letter from Bobby is in my mailbox. I am happy that my October bills are paid and out of my mind for a while. I opened the letter.

Dear Rachel.

I'm sorry to hear that. I know you're not asking for money. I would never think that. We all struggle sometimes. Maybe it's a good time to contact your parents and ask them for help? They love you; you're their daughter. Even if they don't show it, they do love you.

Dear Bobby,

Done. Finished. Not suicidal; just finished. You think you have it bad because you're in jail…? You really don't.

I walk out and mail the letter. I can't believe how calm this guy is about my whole situation, telling me to call my parents. Fuck that.

I make it to the mailbox and slip the letter in. I'm struggling, and he's taking it lightly. No words of encouragement; just call the people who hate me the most next to Stacey and Tyler.

I have no regrets about what I wrote. I am just so angry. All I want is a bottle of vodka. I am so mad. What is one more person mad at me?

It's Halloween night, and the bar is handing out free drinks from 7:00 to 8:00. I don't care about the costume party; I just want free alcohol.

I am already becoming someone who I don't recognize. I have not heard from Bobby in two weeks. I don't really care at this point. All I want is my booze and drunkenness.

I start my way to the bar. I am already a little drunk from the beer I had before I left.

I reach the bar and walk in. It's packed with people dressed up. I sit at a corner table, and the bartender from last time looks at me and puts a beer down in front of me.

"That okay?"

"Yes."

He walks away, and I drink and watch all the other people as they socialize with one another. Two gorillas walk in and take a table next to mine and stare at me. I pay no mind. It is Halloween after all.

I continue my drink as the gorillas stare me down. I get up to go to the bathroom, as the staring makes me uneasy when two females pass my chair.

"Hey, who left these chairs out like this?"

I look over; two girls are asking about who was staring at my chair. I get out of the bathroom line.

"That's my chair actually; sorry. But if it was that big of a thing, then why didn't you just push it in and call it a day?"

The other girl looks at me.

"It's not our job; we have jobs."

I look at them.

"First of all: What does that have to do with anything? Second: What, prostitution?" I laugh.

The blonde girl grabs me by the shirt. I remove her hand and hold it in a fist.

"Come on, bitch. Let's take this outside. I really can take ya!"

I grabbed the chair I pulled out and tried to throw it.

The two gorillas jump in and grab the chair from me. Then they grab me to pull me outside.

When we make it outside, they take off their masks. I am shocked to discover it is Tyler and Stacey.

"Rachel, what the fuck are you doing, man?" Stacey looks at me confused. I look back at her.

"I'm just angry," I confess. "My family hates me, my friends hate me, my boyfriend cheated on me, I'm still jobless, and I don't know where I go from here."

"Stacey, we got to get her home," Tyler says.

They walked me to Stacy's car and put on the backseat with Tyler's arm around me. I am in shock that they still care for me and don't want anything bad to happen.

I grab a bucket that Stacey uses for a trash can and place it in front of my face. I do not trust myself for the alcohol to not come up.

I can't tell what road we are on. I don't care; I just want to get home and sleep. I slouch on Tyler.

"We're almost there," Stacey confirms. "Just another three minutes or so."

I want nothing more than my bed right now. Drinking on an empty stomach was a stupid idea.

We pulled up, and they helped me to my porch.

"I'll take care of Nicki," Tyler says.

I enter my house, and Stacey walks me up to my room and puts me in my bed.

"We got your letters… We can talk in the morning. We'll spend a few hours just to make sure you're okay. We do still care about you… We were just mad and hurting a little."

Tyler comes up.

"Nicki is taken care of. Back to the bar?"

"No, I'm going to spend a few hours here."

Tyler nods his head and walks downstairs to leave.

It is official: I am going down a hill, and it is not the answer. But what else can I do? I am too drunk to think. I get under the blankets and try to sleep.

November

GIVING THANKS TO ALL

I'm awoken the next morning by a knock at my bedroom door. I then saw Stacey and Tyler walk in.

"Hey, I thought you guys left last night."

"We thought about it, but I just decided to spend the night. He just got here."

I look at my clock, it's 1:23 PM. It's the next day—November 1. Everything is a blur from last night.

"We got your letters," Tyler says. "We're sorry about you and Josh. And we're not going to sit here and say we told you so because you already know that. But that's a different story."

"Rachel, listen," Stacey begins. "I'm sorry that you guys got laid off…" She puts her hand on my shoulder. "Trust me, I'm not having an affair with the manager. Trust me on that one."

"I'm sorry that I accused you of it. I was just… I don't know. Angry and upset."

Stacey continues, "I mean, yeah. I think it's weird I didn't get laid off, but I'm thankful I didn't. I wonder why he picked you two. Maybe it's a one-sided thing." Stacey shrugs her shoulders.

"Anyway… Do you remember last night at all?" Tyler asks.

"I remember a fight and being in a car with two gorillas."

"That was us," Stacey says.

"Yeah, I know. Thought that was a hallucination or something…but that was obviously really you, guys."

"Yeah, you left a chair pulled out, and two other blondes got mad at you for it; then you called them prostitutes, and they tried to fight you, and you were all for it!" Tyler laughs as he finishes the story.

"Yeah, then we brought you to the car, and you said that, like, oh, everyone hates you, and you can find a job, and how you are financially unstable right now," Stacey adds.

48

"So here we are giving you $300 right now. We both chipped in," Tyler says.

"Are you okay with October?" Stacey asks.

"Yeah, but now I've got November to come up against…" I reply. "Thanks, guys. This means a lot."

"We're here for you," Stacey tells me.

"Even though we were mad, we didn't want to see you hurt; and we don't want to see you go down this road," Tyler adds. "We care about you. Even when we were mad, we gave a shit."

"I never thought we would talk again," I admit. "Guys, once again… I'm sorry for everything that I either said or didn't say, you know, since all this laid off shit happened."

They both sit on both sides of me on my bed, then back away.

"Go shower up or something," Tyler tells me.

"Are you hung over at all?" Stacey asks.

"A little bit," I reply. "I should get myself out of bed for a bit though. Can I have a truce handshake at least before you leave?"

They both grabbed my hands at once as I put them both out.

"Thanksgiving at my house?" Stacey asks me.

"Why the hell not?"

"Where's my invite?" Tyler asks in a playful way.

"You're going away to fucking Florida."

"Oh, right. I AM. Three weeks from now."

"I'm glad we hatched this all out," Stacey says. "Go take care of yourself and Nicki, then you can get right back in bed. We took care of Nicki last night."

"Are you okay from here?" Tyler asks.

"Yeah, I got it from here."

"Okay. We're out then."

Tyler leaves as Stacey stays behind.

"I know you care about my schooling. Please don't take it personally," she says. "I kind of have a part in that, too. Maybe turn my phone off while I'm busy with school and work. I may not have all the time in the world, but I will always get back to you. And I'm sorry if you ever felt like you couldn't call me. We're homies. Call, text whenever—I'll get back to you. Maybe not right away, but I will eventually. I promise not to get all crazy on you…

"But what are you going to do about November?" she asks.

"I don't know yet," I reply. "I have $300. That's a start."

"Need a place to stay, you know I have an extra room," she offers.

"You know I don't like doing that shit though."

"I know. But as a last resort, just give it a thought."

Stacey gets up from the floor and leaves the room.

"Love ya, text me!" she says.

I go downstairs, and Nicki is waiting at the door. I let him out and prepared to wash up from last night's events. I really appreciate the money and the offer. Maybe this is my last resort after all. It's a new month, and I am out of options. My aunt's savings aren't enough for all the bills even.

It's Thanksgiving, and I pull into Stacey's driveway and start my way up to the front door. For the first time in months, I have no anxiety about seeing someone. Her dad opens the door.

"Hey! Nice to see you again around here."

He leaves the door open, and I walk in. Stacey's two little sisters run up and hug my leg like they haven't seen me in ten years.

"Your sister has been very busy lately, that's why you haven't seen me in a decade!" I tell them.

Stacey comes from the kitchen.

"Hi! Welcome! And happy Thanksgiving!"

"Same to you."

"Foods already done. We're just waiting for our dad to get it out." He sets the table with the food, and we all take a seat. Her dad sits down last.

"We all have to tell what we're thankful for before we eat. I'll start. I'm thankful for my wonderful three daughters and the fact that I have the strength every day to take care of them. Also for my jobs I have to support them and keep them fed."

"I guess it's my turn to go…?" Stacey says. "Okay, my job also; and my friends, my family, and my schooling. I have a lot of opportunities that some don't."

Awkwardness sets in as everyone turns to me.

"My friends and my home. That's all I can really say." My phone then rings. "Excuse me…" I say. It's Chris, my brother-in-law. I pick it up in the other room just as it stops ringing. I wait for a voicemail to come through. It takes a few seconds, but one finally comes through. I pick it up and listen to it.

"Hey Rachel, it's Chris. Your niece was just born about 35 minutes ago, so you want to come down? You know where to find us. Room 303 in the maternity clinic."

I hung it up and went back to the table.

"My niece was just born."

"Oh my God, congrats Aunt Rachel!" Stacey puts her arm around me as her dad shakes my hand.

"They had the nerve to invite me now."

"Do you wanna go down now? I can drive you."

"Yeah, Stacey can drive you," her dad says.

"But I just got here."

"You should be there though," Stacey's dad says. "I know all about this situation, and you need to go. As awkward as it is."

"You're right," I say in a low voice.

"I'm going to make some plates," he says. "One for you, and two for your sister and brother-in-law."

Stacey gets ready as her dad prepares plates and puts them in a bag with all the basics.

"Here you go!" he tells me. "Happy Thanksgiving." "Also, congrats."

Stacey is already out of the house, waiting to take me.

The roads are empty. I have so much anxiety about seeing my family, more than I had from when I first met Bobby in his jail back in June. The hospital is a short six-minute ride. Stacey can tell that I have anxiety and stays silent.

We reach the hospital, and she pulls into the clinic's main doors. She puts the car into park.

"Okay. This is it. Breathe."

I breathe along with Stacy as she guides me through the deep breath technique, then I get out and start my way to the main doors. I'm greeted by the desk person.

"Maternity, room 303? I'm here to visit my sister Rose Becker. My niece was just born. This is just food from my dinner I just had, that's all."

I'm sent up to the third floor without a word to me. I go up in the elevator and step off on the floor where my sister is. I place myself against the wall, as I know what I'm in for. I take one more deep breath and then walk the walk of fear as I reach her room. I don't even hesitate to walk right in.

All eyes are on me as I walk in.

"Hello, guys. Happy Thanksgiving to everyone."

I get stared at as my mother comes over and hugs me. My father's look is full of hate.

"Come say hi to your daughter, Jason." He comes over and puts his hand on my shoulders. "I hope that we can be a happy family now." My mom gives him a hand gesture to leave the room.

I am left with just my sister and Chris, along with their daughter.

"So how was the delivery?"

"Rough and tough," Chris says.

"I brought you some food for both of you, along with mine." They take it and unwrap it. "I'm sorry we couldn't be on good terms through all of this…"

Rose puts her hand up.

"It's both our faults. Meet Miracle Faith Becker."

I look in the glass part as she sleeps.

"She's beautiful. A combo of both of you. Can I hold her?"

"Sure, that's fine," Rose responds. "She's sleeping, but she just ate anyway, so maybe she'll be okay."

I picked her up and looked at her. This little girl needs her aunt in her life as a positive role model next to her parents. Not some drunk asshole who she would grow up telling people that her aunt is—or was—a drunk.

My parents walked back in with cafeteria food.

"No food for us?" my dad laughs. It is still awkward, but I didn't want to ruin this moment.

"Who made these plates?" Chris asks. "They're really good."

"My friend's dad. I was over, and her dad made all this food from scratch pretty much." "He's an amazing cook!" Chris says. "Tell him thank you do much with a capital T!" "This is amazing!" Rose agrees.

The five of us sit and eat whatever food we have in silence.

A nurse comes into the room.

"Hey, uh, visiting hours are over," she tells us.

"Okay, we'll be out," my dad says. "Rachel, need a ride home?"

"Yeah, kind of," I reply.

"Thanks for coming, and happy Thanksgiving!" my sister says. "Rachel, I want to talk like we used to."

I hugged her and Chris both, then walked out with my parents.

We get into my dad's car, and we sit there for a minute in complete awkwardness.

"You're our daughter, and we love you, Rachel," my dad says. "Maybe we did handle that whole situation wrong."

"We want you to come over for Christmas," my mom adds, "and you can even invite your friends if you want. We like them. You said Stacey, right?"

"I was invited for dinner at her house, yeah."

"Yeah, come over to our Christmas Eve gathering, and bring her along."

"Can my friend Bobby come also? He's another good friend."

"The more the merrier." He starts up the car and pulls out of the garage.

We arrived home, and I looked at my parents.

"It was nice seeing you again, Rachel, after all this time," my mom says. "Christmas Eve? See you then?"

I nod my head and smile.

"Yes."

They pull off.

I go inside, completely exhausted. I put Stacey and Tyler in a group text.

Hey, sorry to bother you right now, but I just met my niece, and every-thing went great. We discussed things, and it went good. Thanks for dinner, by the way, Stacey.

I don't even care that I am alone for the rest of the night. I am just happy to have everybody in my life back. Now all I need is a job.

My letter from Bobby sits in my mail pile.

Happy Thanksgiving. I know this is a lot. I will not take that last letter personally. I hope by now in the past few weeks you are okay now.

I know I was wrong in that last letter, and it takes a lot of pride to admit that. I start the next letter with an apology:

Dear Bobby,

I went down a hill of alcoholism for about a month. I'm sorry. I met my niece tonight and saw my parents. I'm going over there for Christmas Eve next month. I asked if you could come, and they said you're more than welcome!

I set it in the mailbox for the mailman to take tomorrow. I trust him enough to get it where it needs to be. I mean, the other letters did when they were in his possession. I turn on the TV and sit down with the rest of my food. This Thanksgiving, I have more to be thankful for: family, friends, and food on the table every night, while some people don't even have a meal or a bed. My life right now isn't the best—but it's not the hardest either.

December

CHRISTMAS

It's the twenty-third. Bobby comes home today. I stand outside of the prison, waiting with a sign, along with Tyler and Stacey. I wait and stare intently at the main doors with excitement and nervousness at the same time.

The doors open, and I see Bobby in the distance in a white tee and black pants. His face glows up with happiness when he sees me. I dropped the sign and ran up and hugged him like I had known him for years.

"HEY RACHEL! It's so nice to see you!" He hugs me with his strong, muscular arms. The same arms that held a gun up to an elderly couple that night.

"We thought you could use a ride home, and also a surprise."

Tyler and Stacey walk up and give him handshakes with sincere grins. I think they are so speechless; they can't find the words to say.

"Where you heading to?" I ask.

"Uh, I don't really know…" he answers.

"Come stay with me for a few days," I offer. "You're already spending Christmas with my family, along with these guys. I live alone, so it's totally okay with my parents!" I joke.

We all gather in my car and start our way back into the world.

"How's it feel to be out?" Tyler asks.

"FREE. Let's just leave it at that!"

"You're not such a bad guy after all," Stacey admits.

"Let's get of here," I say. I start up the car and drive off the prison's property.

"Oh, by the way, Tyler, thanks for giving Rachel a ride over the summer to visit," Bobby says.

I look at Stacy in my rearview mirror.

"No…problem," Tyler says.

We reach my house. Bobby is the first one out of the car.

"Nice place you got," he says.

55

"I should get going," Stacey says in a disappointed voice. "Bobby congrats on your release. Stay out of trouble now!"

"I will trust me."

Stacey gives me a wave and gets in her car.

"Sticking around Ty?"

"Nah, I want you two to get more acquainted. Nice seeing you out, man. See you tomorrow night for the Christmas Eve party?"

"Yes, be there at 6:00." Both go their separate ways.

Bobby and I walk up to my porch, and I unlock my door. Nicki sniffs Bobby as soon as he walks in.

"That's Nicki. He's friendly." Bobby bends down and gives him a scruff. "So, any food or drink you would like?"

"Look, I just want some liquor."

I pour him a glass and sit next to him on the couch. I go in my drawer and take out a stack of letters.

"You kept them all?" Bobby says with wide eyes. He then goes in his bag and brings out his stack. "Even the mean, one I kept. So do your parents know about me?"

"You're a friend from work at Royals, okay? It isn't my place to tell them your business."

"So, if I may ask, why are Tyler and Stacey coming?"

"Tyler's parents really don't care where he goes, as he doesn't really celebrate it. As for Stacy, we made a deal. I went to her house for Thanksgiving, so she's coming for Christmas at my family's. And yes, my sister is gonna be there. So glad we hatched things out!"

"So Tyler lives with his parents and brother?" he asks.

"And Stacey lives with her dad and two sisters. Her mom walked out on her when she was born," I explain.

"Oh wow, that's rough."

"Yeah, I can't imagine. I can understand how she feels, but I don't know how she feels, you know?"

"Yeah, I totally get that." Bobby pauses for a moment, then says: "It's going to be so weird. No more letters in the mail to look for. But I'm here in person, so that's even cooler! Where do I sleep?"

"Guest room upstairs," I say. "Don't tell me you're going to sleep now!"

"It's been three years of a hard bed. I want a soft bed now."

"I get it," I say in response. "Okay, sleep tight."

Bobby takes his wine and goes upstairs.

It's Christmas Eve day. I prepare to see my family as Bobby prepares to meet my family. Bobby comes out of the bathroom.

"How do I look?"

I glance over at him.

"Really nice," I admit. "But a suit with a candy cane tie though?"

"Yeah, I went out last night to the store down the street to go pick something up. You know, at that thrift shop? Wanted to look nice for your family."

"I appreciate that." I look at my phone. There's a group text from Tyler and Stacey. "Looks like we'll be the last ones there, Bobby," I say. "Everyone is already there. Even my friends!"

"Do they know about y'all's fight?"

"No, they don't. Let's it keep it that way."

"You got it, Rach."

"I just don't want them to think differently of them."

We pull up with everybody already there. I take a deep breath and look at Bobby.

"Let's go."

We went out and walked in the front door. I'm greeted by my parents, and they hug me.

"You must be Bobby."

"We heard a lot about you what a great friend you are to our Rachel."

"Yes, she took me under her wing. Merry Christmas!" he says as he hugs my parents. Tyler and Stacy come over to greet Bobby, too. "Merry Christmas, guys."

"Same to you!" Tyler shakes his hand as Stacey waves and smiles.

I saw Rose on the couch with Chris. I walk over by myself and look at her. Bobby follows a second later.

"Must be your niece. May I?" He puts up his arms.

"Sure." Rose hands Miracle over to Bobby. He looks at her. "I hope to have my own someday. She's gorgeous." He hands Miracle back to Rose.

I step out to where Tyler and Stacey are. Bobby comes out along with me.

"Rachel, can I talk to you for a second?" He takes me aside and takes an envelope out of his pocket. I open it. It's $3,000. "It's the money for college. Merry Christmas. You're going to have the best years at college, and I want to hear all about them. I took it out of my sister's death money."

"She's proud right now," I said.

"You know things will turn around if you let THEM."

I look at him confused. Tyler and Stacey come over. Tyler breaks the silence.

"So, we were thinking… how would the two of you like to be roommates with us? I mean, we can help with the bills and all."

"We can be like the *Three's Company*," Stacey adds.

"Only difference is, I'm really gay," Tyler finishes.

Bobby says he's moving in with his dad.

"So, after the holidays?"

"Until one of us gets engaged or something, why not?" I look at Stacy. "Any words from you?"

"I like the idea. But do you, Rachel?"

I nod my head with a smile.

"I really do. Let's do it after in the following week or so, before New Year's Eve. Because I can help as soon as possible."

We go in, and everybody is at the table. I whisper to Bobby, "That's what you meant."

Bobby nods his head.

"Yep."

I remain standing as the rest sit.

"Everybody? Can I have your attention? I want to make a toast." My dad passes champagne glasses to everyone, along with the bottle. As everyone pours themself a glass, I prepare for my speech. Suddenly, everybody's glasses are full, and all eyes are on me.

"I want to say a few words about life… As we grow up, we realize even that one person who wasn't supposed to let us down probably will. You'll get your heart broken, and you'll break others. You'll fight with your family, soulmate, your best friend, or even fall in love with them…

"Always come back to them. And you'll cry, because life is flying by. So, laugh too much, take too many pictures, love like you've never been hurt, and forgive freely, even if they're wrong. Tell someone off; tell someone what they mean to you. But most importantly: Live in the moment. Live life to the fullest. Because each second of anger is a chance of happiness you'll never get back.

"In a closing line I love you all, and Merry Christmas." I raise my glass. "To family and friends."

Everybody raises their glasses and repeats it. I sit with applause from the table.

"You did amazing with that speech.!" Tyler says.

The food gets passed around with chatter and laughs.

"Spring, your journey starts," Bobby reminds me.

"I can't wait!" I say.   "Everything falls into place with time," Bobby says.

I glance around at everyone. At one point or another, they were all estranged with me. Bobby kept me sane for the past nine months. I wouldn't mind having Bobby as a life lasting friend. Things are starting to look up as things are going back to the way they used to be and that's the way they should be. Bobby looks over at me. "Things will be easier from here." 'I smile at him. "They already have" "Just know Rachel you are never alone and don't ever think you are." "Also, what's your major?' I know you said law but what job in the law field exactly?" I shrug my shoulders. "Not really sure to be honest with you want to explore the jobs first before deciding." "But I know it will be in that career though." "But for now, let's enjoy each other. Bobby was no longer a criminal or a pen-pal he was a friend and I hope it always stays that way.